P9-CTP-548

Animal Time

Just Right Cat

Time to Read® is an early reader program designed to guide children to literacy success regardless of age or grade level. The program's three levels correspond to stages of reading readiness, making book selection straightforward, and assuring that when it's time for a child to read, the right book is waiting.

Level 1	**Beginning to Read**	• Large, simple type • Basic vocabulary	• Word repetition • Strong illustration support
Level 2	**Reading with Help**	• Short sentences • Engaging stories	• Simple dialogue • Illustration support
Level 3	**Reading Independently**	• Longer sentences • Harder words	• Short paragraphs • Increased story complexity

For Jameson, who is just right—LHH

To all the wonderful staff at Favours Day Nursery, Moulton. Thank you.—AW

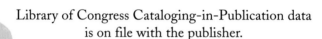

Library of Congress Cataloging-in-Publication data
is on file with the publisher.

Text copyright © 2020 by Lori Haskins Houran
Illustrations copyright © 2020 by Albert Whitman & Company
Illustrations by Alex Willmore
First published in the United States of America
in 2020 by Albert Whitman & Company
ISBN 978-0-8075-7196-5 (hardcover)
ISBN 978-0-8075-7194-1 (ebook)

Printed in China
10 9 8 7 6 5 4 3 2 1 RRD 24 23 22 21 20

Designed by Valerie Hernández

TIME TO READ® is a registered trademark
of Albert Whitman & Company.
For more information about Albert Whitman & Company,
visit our website at www.albertwhitman.com.

Animal Time

Just Right Cat

Lori Haskins Houran

illustrated by
Alex Willmore

Albert Whitman & Company
Chicago, Illinois

Cat wants to be big.

Big like Dad.

But Cat is small.

Too small.

Cat wants to be loud.

Loud like Dad.

But Cat is soft.

Too soft.

Too small.
Too soft.
Too bad for Cat.

Who's that?
A *tiny* cat!

Dad wants to help.
But he is big.
Too big.

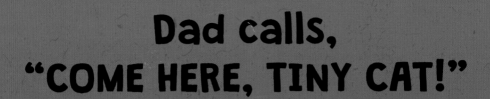

Dad calls,
"COME HERE, TINY CAT!"

But he is loud.
Too loud.

Too big.
Too loud.
Too bad for Dad.

"Let me help," says Cat.

Cat is small.

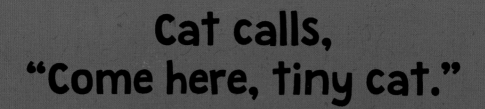

Cat calls,
"Come here, tiny cat."

Cat is soft.

Cat is just right!

Big.

Small.

Tiny.

Just right.